THE WIND IN THE WILLOWS

By KENNETH GRAHAME   RETOLD BY G. C. BARRETT   ILLUSTRATED BY DON DAILY

COURAGE
BOOKS

AN IMPRINT OF RUNNING PRESS
PHILADELPHIA · LONDON

CONTENTS

*Don Daily dedicates the illustrations
in this book to his Aunt Anna*

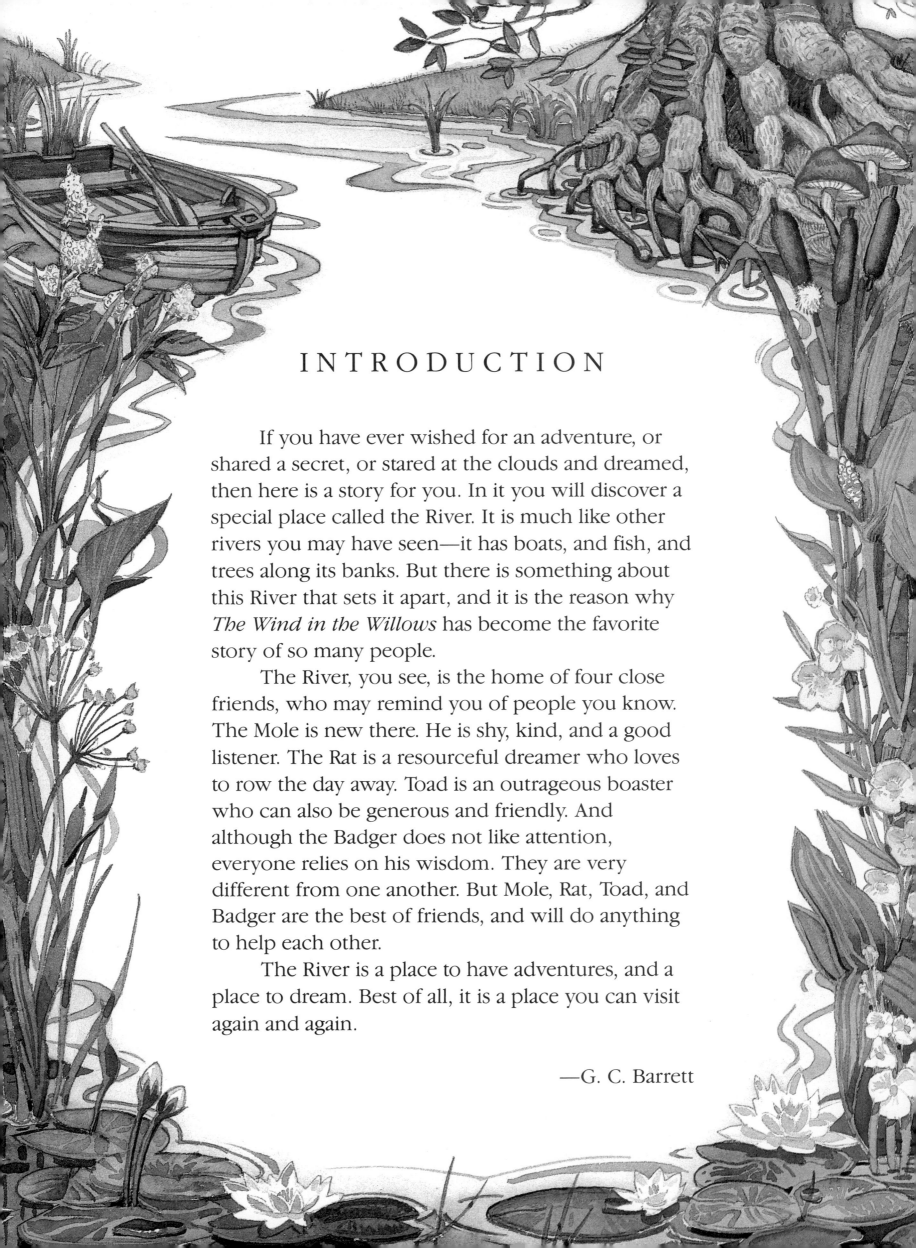

INTRODUCTION

If you have ever wished for an adventure, or shared a secret, or stared at the clouds and dreamed, then here is a story for you. In it you will discover a special place called the River. It is much like other rivers you may have seen—it has boats, and fish, and trees along its banks. But there is something about this River that sets it apart, and it is the reason why *The Wind in the Willows* has become the favorite story of so many people.

The River, you see, is the home of four close friends, who may remind you of people you know. The Mole is new there. He is shy, kind, and a good listener. The Rat is a resourceful dreamer who loves to row the day away. Toad is an outrageous boaster who can also be generous and friendly. And although the Badger does not like attention, everyone relies on his wisdom. They are very different from one another. But Mole, Rat, Toad, and Badger are the best of friends, and will do anything to help each other.

The River is a place to have adventures, and a place to dream. Best of all, it is a place you can visit again and again.

—G. C. Barrett

The River Bank

The Mole had been working very hard all morning long, spring-cleaning his little home—first with brooms, then with a pail of whitewash, till he had dust in his throat and spots on his black fur. Spring was in the air above, and all was restless. It was small wonder, then, that the Mole suddenly flung down his brush and said "Forget spring cleaning!" Something up above was calling him powerfully.

Without even putting on his coat, he scraped and scrabbled through his steep little tunnel. At last, *pop!* his snout came out into the sunlight, and he found himself rolling in the warm grass of a great meadow.

"This is fine!" he said to himself. The sun struck warm on his fur. Jumping up joyfully, he rambled busily across the meadow. It all seemed too good to be true. Everywhere he found birds building nests, flowers budding, animals rushing about.

4

Everything was happy. Instead of hearing his conscience whisper "whitewash!" he felt jolly.

He thought his happiness was complete when he suddenly found himself by the edge of a river. Never in his life had he seen a river. It was like a sleek, winding animal, chasing and chuckling, gripping things with a gurgle and then leaving them with a laugh. It gleamed and sparkled. The Mole trotted along the river, spellbound. When he finally tired, he sat on the bank. The river chattered on, as if telling him the best stories in the world.

As he sat on the grass, a dark hole in the opposite bank caught his eye. Something bright seemed to shine in it like a tiny star. Then it winked at him. It was an eye. A face grew around it—a serious little brown face, with whiskers, small neat ears, and thick silky hair.

It was the Water Rat! The two animals stood and observed each other cautiously.

"Hello, Mole!" said the Water Rat.

"Hello, Rat!" said the Mole.

"Would you like to come over?" asked the Rat after a moment. He stepped into a little boat which the Mole had not seen. It was just the right size for two animals.

The Rat rowed quickly across. He held out his paw. "Now, step lively!" he said. The Mole took the Rat's paw and found himself seated in the stern of a real boat.

"I've never been in a boat before," said the Mole.

"What?" cried the Water Rat. "Believe me, there is *nothing* half so much worth doing as simply messing about in boats," he said dreamily. "Just—messing—about. Say, I have an idea. Suppose we go down the river!"

The Mole wiggled his toes from sheer happiness. "Let's start at once!"

The Rat pulled up beside his hole, climbed in, and reappeared with a fat picnic basket. He shoved it under the seat and climbed back into the boat.

"What's inside it?" asked the Mole.

"Cold chicken," replied the Rat. "Coldhamcoldroastbeefsaladfrenchrollswatercresssandwichesgingeralesodawaterlemonade—"

"This is too much!" cried the Mole in ecstacy.

The Rat rowed silently for some time. The Mole dreamed and trailed his paw in the water.

"So this is a river!" the Mole said at last.

"*The* River," corrected the Rat. "I live by it and with it and in it. It's my world, and I don't want any other. What it hasn't got is not worth having."

"What lies over *there*?" asked the Mole, waving a paw toward a distant woodland on one side of the river.

"That? Oh, that's just the Wild Wood," said the Rat shortly. "We don't go there much."

"They aren't very *nice* people in there?" said the Mole nervously.

"W-e-ll," replied the Rat, "There's Badger, of course, he wouldn't live anywhere else. Dear old Badger!—But there—are others," explained the Rat. "Like the weasels. You can't trust them, and that's a fact.

"Now then!" said the Rat. "Here's where we're going to lunch."

The Rat helped the still-awkward Mole ashore. They spread the tablecloth on the grass, and when all was ready, they ate.

Halfway through dessert, there was a sudden rustle in the bushes behind them, and a stripy head, with high shoulders behind it, peered forth.

"Come on, Badger!" shouted the Rat.

The Badger trotted forward a pace or two. "Hm! Company!" he grunted. He turned his back and disappeared from view.

"That's the sort of fellow he is," observed the disappointed Rat. "He dislikes social life."

Just then a boat came into view on the river. The rower—a short, stout figure—was splashing water everywhere, and his boat was rolling dangerously from side to side. The Rat stood up and waved, but the Toad shook his head and worked the oars even harder.

8

"He'll fall out of that boat in a minute," said the Rat. The Toad disappeared around the bend.

The Rat noted, quietly, that they ought to be moving. Packing the picnic basket was not as pleasant as unpacking it. It never is. But the Mole was enjoying everything that day.

The afternoon sun was getting low as the Rat sculled gently homewards, murmuring poetry to himself. He invited Mole into his comfortable home, and told stories of the River—thrilling stories about floods, and fishing, and trips. When the Mole became sleepy, the considerate Rat escorted him upstairs to the best bedroom. There the Mole laid his head on the pillow with great contentment, knowing that his new-found friend the River was lapping below the window.

This day was the first of many great days for the Mole. He learned to swim and to row. And with his ear near the willow branches, he sometimes caught something of what the wind went whispering among them.

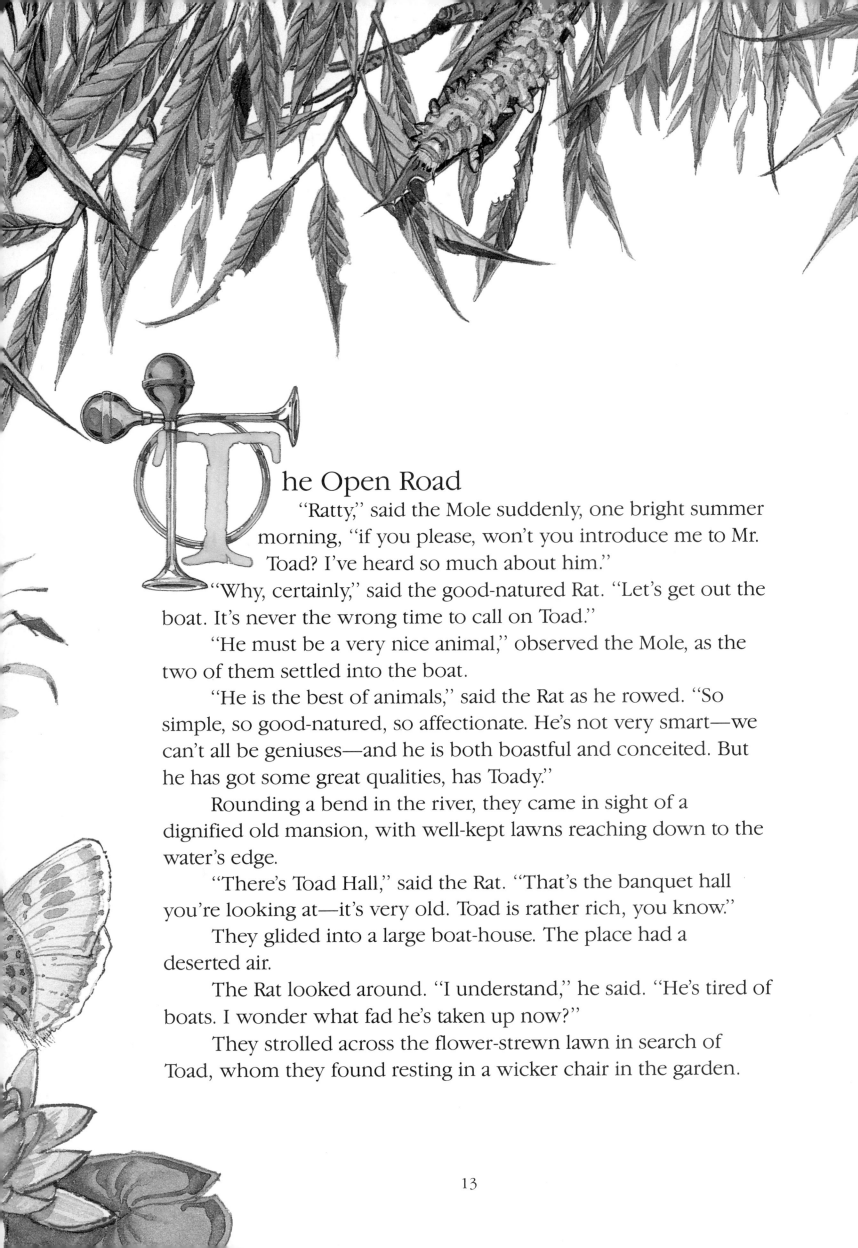

The Open Road

"Ratty," said the Mole suddenly, one bright summer morning, "if you please, won't you introduce me to Mr. Toad? I've heard so much about him."

"Why, certainly," said the good-natured Rat. "Let's get out the boat. It's never the wrong time to call on Toad."

"He must be a very nice animal," observed the Mole, as the two of them settled into the boat.

"He is the best of animals," said the Rat as he rowed. "So simple, so good-natured, so affectionate. He's not very smart—we can't all be geniuses—and he is both boastful and conceited. But he has got some great qualities, has Toady."

Rounding a bend in the river, they came in sight of a dignified old mansion, with well-kept lawns reaching down to the water's edge.

"There's Toad Hall," said the Rat. "That's the banquet hall you're looking at—it's very old. Toad is rather rich, you know."

They glided into a large boat-house. The place had a deserted air.

The Rat looked around. "I understand," he said. "He's tired of boats. I wonder what fad he's taken up now?"

They strolled across the flower-strewn lawn in search of Toad, whom they found resting in a wicker chair in the garden.

A large map was spread out on his knees.

"Hooray!" he cried, jumping up on seeing them. He shook their paws warmly, never waiting to be introduced to Mole. "I was just going to send a boat down the river for you," he went on, dancing round them.

The Mole made a polite remark about Toad's "delightful residence."

"Finest house on the River," cried Toad boisterously. "Or anywhere else," he could not help adding.

The Rat nudged the Mole. Unfortunately, the Toad saw him do it, and turned very red. Then Toad burst out laughing.

"All right, Ratty," he said. "It's only my way, you know. Now, look here. You have got to help me. I've given up boating," Toad said with disgust. "It's silly amusement. No, I've discovered the real thing. Come and see!"

Toad led them to the stables. There they found a gypsy wagon, shining new.

"There's real life for you!" cried the Toad, puffing himself with pride. "This wagon represents the open road. Travel! Excitement! The whole world before you! And this is the best cart that can be built. Planned it all myself, I did!"

The Mole was tremendously excited, but the Rat just snorted and thrust his hands into his pockets. The wagon was very comfortable. There were little sleeping-bunks, a stove, a table that folded up against the wall, and lockers filled with food.

"All complete!" said the Toad triumphantly. "You'll find everything you'll need, when we start this afternoon."

"I beg your pardon," said the Rat slowly, "but did you say 'we'?"

"Dear old Ratty," said Toad, imploringly,

"you've *got* to come. I can't possibly manage without you. You don't want to stay on the dull old River all your life, do you? I want to show you the world!"

"I'm not coming," said the Rat. "I like the River just fine. And Mole's going to stick with me, aren't you, Mole?"

"It sounds as if it might be—well, rather fun!" said Mole wistfully. He had fallen in love with the wagon, and the Rat could see it. The Rat could not bear to disappoint his friends.

The triumphant Toad harnessed his old gray horse to the wagon, and they set off, all talking at once. It was a golden afternoon.

Late in the evening, tired and happy and miles from home, they stopped at a remote clearing. There they ate a simple supper. As they talked, a yellow moon came to keep them company, and the stars grew fuller and larger all around them. At last they climbed into their little bunks in the wagon.

The next day, they had a pleasant ramble. They traveled
down narrow country lanes, and it was not until afternoon that
they came out onto a main road.

They were strolling along pleasantly, Toad talking nonstop,
when they heard a faint hum, like a distant bee. Glancing back,
they saw a cloud of dust. Out of the dust came a faint
"*poop-poop*!"

Suddenly the peaceful scene changed. With a blast of wind
and a whirl of sound, it was upon them! They had a moment's
glimpse of a magnificent motor car. It roared by, flinging a cloud of
dust around the wagon. They jumped for the nearest ditch. The
"*poop-poop*!" rang like a shout in their ears.

Startled, the old gray horse reared up, and drove the cart
backwards to the deep ditch on the side of the road. The wagon
teetered on the edge, and then crashed down onto its side.

The Rat hopped up and down as the car disappeared. "You villain!" he shouted after it. "You road-hog!"

Toad sat in the middle of the road, staring in the direction of the motor car. He wore a dreamy expression.

"Glorious!" Toad whispered. "The *real* way to travel—the *only* way to travel! When I speed in my motor car, dust clouds will spring up behind me!"

"There is nothing we can do," said the Rat to the Mole. "He has a new craze. Come on—we shall just have to walk to town."

They had not gone far when Toad caught up with them.

"I'm done with carts forever," said Toad. "My friends, thank you for coming on this journey. If it had not been for you, I would never have seen that magnificent motor car!"

The Rat glanced at the Mole in despair as they trudged toward town. There they boarded a train that took them to the station near Toad Hall. They put the spellbound Toad to bed, and at a very late hour Mole and Rat sat down to supper in their little riverside home.

The next evening the Mole was sitting on the bank, fishing, when the Rat came strolling by.

"Hear the news?" Rat said. "Everyone's talking about it. Toad went to town early this morning. He's ordered a large and very expensive motor car."

The Wild Wood

The Mole had long wanted to make the acquaintance of the Badger. But whenever the Mole mentioned his wish to the Rat, the Rat would say, "Badger'll turn up some day. I'll introduce you then."

The Mole had to be content with this. But the Badger never came. Before Mole knew it, summer was long over. Cold and frost kept Mole and Rat indoors, and the Mole's thoughts turned again to the solitary gray Badger.

One afternoon, when the Rat was dozing in his armchair before the fire, the Mole decided to go by himself to the Wild Wood and strike up an acquaintance with Mr. Badger.

It was a cold, still afternoon with a hard steely sky overhead when he slipped out of the warm parlor into the open air. The country lay bare around him. Without green leaves, everything

looked poor. But Mole found it exhilarating. He pushed on towards the Wild Wood, which lay before him low and threatening, like a black reef in a dark sea.

He walked further into the woods, where the light was less, and the trees crouched nearer and nearer.

Everything was very still now. Dusk approached suddenly. The light was draining away like floodwater.

Then the faces began.

Over his shoulder Mole thought he saw a face: a little evil wedge-shaped face, looking out at him from a hole. When he turned, the thing had vanished.

He told himself cheerfully not to imagine things. He passed another hole, and another, and another; and then— *yes!*—*no!*—*yes!* he saw a narrow face with hard eyes flash up for an instant from a hole and then disappear. He hesitated. Then every hole, near and far— and there were hundreds of them—seemed to possess a face. They stared with hatred: all hard-eyed and evil and sharp.

If he could only get away from the holes, he thought, there would be no more faces. He jumped off the path and plunged into the woods. Then the whistling began—very faint, and far behind him. He ran on. Then still very faint and shrill, it sounded far ahead of him. He stopped. Then it broke out on either side of him. He was alone and far from help, and night was closing in.

As he paused, a rabbit came running hard towards him through the trees. The animal almost brushed him as it dashed past. "Get out of here, you fool!" the rabbit squeaked. Then he was gone.

In panic, the Mole ran, he knew
not where. He fell many times. At last, too
tired to run, he took refuge in the deep hollow
of an old beech tree, hoping he was safe.

Meanwhile, the Rat dozed by his fireside. Then a log slipped,
the fire crackled, and he woke up with a start. The house was very
quiet, and he called out "Moly!" But the Mole was not there.

The Rat left the house and examined the muddy ground
outside. He could see the Mole's footprints, running along the
River and directly into the Wild Wood.

The Rat looked very grave and stood in thought for a minute
or two. Then he entered the house, strapped on a pair of pistols,
took up a sturdy stick, and set off to find his friend.

Darkness was coming on as he entered the Wood. He called
out "Moly! Moly! Where are you? It's me, Ratty!" He plunged
deeper into the woods, calling as he went.

After an hour, he heard an answering cry. From out of an old
beech tree came a feeble voice, saying, "Ratty! Is that really you?"

The Rat crept into the hollow, where he found the Mole, exhausted and trembling.

"I've been so frightened!" stuttered the Mole. "O, I'm so sorry!"

"I understand," said the Rat soothingly. "But you shouldn't have done it, Moly. We river-bankers hardly ever come here by ourselves. You have to be careful if you're small."

The Rat decided to let the Mole rest a while. After a time, the Rat said, "Now then! We really must go." He went to the entrance and put his head out.

"What's up, Ratty?" asked the Mole.

"*Snow* is up," replied the Rat briefly. "Or rather, *down.* It's snowing hard. Well, it can't be helped. Only thing is, I don't know exactly where we are. And this snow makes everything look so different."

The Mole would not have known that it was the same forest. They set out bravely, holding onto each other. But every tree looked the same. Soon they were weary, wet, and chilled to the bone. There seemed to be no way out.

They struggled on, and passed around the side of a little hill. Suddenly, the Mole tripped and fell on his face with a squeal.

"O my leg!" he cried. "O my poor shin!"

"Poor old Mole!" said the Rat kindly. "Let's have a look." He took out a handkerchief and dabbed at the Mole's shin.

"You've got a little cut. It's a very clean cut," said the Rat, looking closely. "This was not done by a stick or stump. Looks as if it was made by a sharp edge, like something metal." The Rat began to scratch in the snow.

Suddenly the Rat cried "Hooray!" and bounced up. "Hooray-oo-ray-oo-ray-oo-ray!"

"What *is* it?" asked the Mole, still nursing his leg.

"Come and see!" said the delighted Rat, as he danced a jig.

The Mole bent down to look. "All I see is a doormat," he said.

"Don't you see what it *means*?" cried the Rat. "Help me shovel!" They both shoveled the snow with their paws. In a few moments they saw a wonderful sight.

In the side of the snowbank was a solid-looking little door. A bell-pull hung by its side, and below it, on an engraved brass plate, they could read:

MR. BADGER

The Mole fell backwards on the snow from sheer surprise and delight.

"Rat! You're so clever! I got a cut, and you found what cut me. Then you found this doormat and reasoned there must be a door to go with it. . . ."

"Are we going to sit in the snow all night?" interrupted the Rat. "Ring the bell!"

While the Rat hammered the door, the Mole swung on the bell-pull with all his might. And from a long way off, they heard a deep-toned bell respond.

Mr. Badger

They waited patiently for what seemed a very long time, stamping in the snow to keep their feet warm. At last they heard slow shuffling footsteps approaching the door.

There was a noise as the bolt shot back. The door opened a few inches, enough to show a long snout and a pair of sleepy blinking eyes.

"Who is it, disturbing people on such a night?" said a gruff and suspicious voice. "Speak up!"

"O, Badger," cried the Rat, "let us in, please. It's me, Rat, and my friend Mole. We've lost our way."

"Why, Ratty!" exclaimed the Badger in a much friendlier

voice. "Come in, both of you. Lost in the snow! And in the Wild Wood, too! Come in."

The two animals tumbled over each other in their eagerness to get inside. The Badger looked down on them kindly and said, "This is not a night for small animals to be out. Come with me to the kitchen."

The Badger shuffled down a long, gloomy passage, and Rat and Mole followed. Badger flung open a door, and they found themselves in the warmth of a large firelit kitchen.

The kindly Badger thrust them down in front of the fire. He fetched dry robes and slippers for them. Then he bandaged Mole's shin as good as new. The frightening Wild Wood seemed miles away.

The Badger summoned them to the table to eat. He sat in his armchair and nodded gravely as Rat and Mole told their story. He never said "I told you so," or remarked that they should have done so-and-so. The Mole began to feel very friendly towards him.

When supper was finished, the Badger said heartily, "Now then! Tell me the news from the River. How's old Toad?"

"From bad to worse," said the Rat gravely. "Another wreck just last week. He insists on driving, and nobody can teach him anything."

"How many has he had?" inquired the Badger gloomily.

"Wrecks, or cars?" asked the Rat. "Well, they're the same thing with Toad. This is the seventh so far."

"He's been in the hospital three times," added the Mole. "I'm worried all the time."

"Badger, we're his friends!" said the Rat. "Shouldn't we do something?"

The Badger went through a bit of hard thinking. "I can't do anything *now*." Rat and Mole knew that most animals did nothing strenuous during the winter. They were sleepy, and rested away the cold days and nights. The Badger stroked his chin and continued: "*But*, when the days are longer, we'll go to Toad and tell him we'll take no nonsense. We'll make him a sensible Toad!" He smiled reassuringly at the Mole.

"Well, it's time for bed," said the Badger, taking his candlestick from the mantelpiece. "Come along, you two, and I'll show you to your quarters."

The next morning, Mole took the opportunity to tell Badger how comfortable his home seemed.

"You know how it is," said the Mole. "Once you're underground, nothing can hurt you. Things go on overhead, and you let 'em. When you want to, up you go, and there the things are, waiting for you."

"That's exactly what I say," the Badger replied, beaming. He lighted a lantern and motioned the Mole to follow him. They passed through a hall and down a large tunnel. Mole was staggered at the size of Badger's home. There were passages and rooms everywhere, with stone pillars and arches. There were even vaulted storehouses as big as Toad's banquet hall.

"Badger, how did you ever build all this?" wondered the Mole aloud.

"I did none of it," said the Badger simply. "I only cleaned out rooms as I needed them. You see, very long ago, on the spot where the Wild Wood now stands, there was a city—a city of humans. Here they lived, and talked, and walked, and slept. They were powerful and built things to last, for they thought their city would last forever."

"What has become of them all?" asked the Mole.

"Who can tell?" said the Badger. "People come, they stay for a while—and then they go. It is their way. But we animals remain.

There were badgers here long before that city ever came to be. And now there are badgers here again. We may move out, but we wait, and then back we come. And so will it ever be."

The Rat was anxious to start for the River, so the Badger took up his lantern again. Rat and Mole followed him through a stuffy tunnel that wound and dipped for what seemed miles. At last daylight began to show itself through a tangle of roots. Badger bid them a hasty goodbye, pushed them through the opening, and then retreated, closing the hole off again with dead leaves and hanging roots.

Mole and Rat found themselves on the very edge of the Wild Wood. In front of them was a great space of quiet fields, and far ahead, the glint of the River. The wintry sun hung red and low on the horizon.

Pausing to look back, Mole saw the Wild Wood, menacing and dark in the snow. Then he turned and with his friend hiked swiftly toward home, knowing that the gentle River and fields held adventure enough, in their own way, to last a lifetime.

Mr. Toad

One bright morning in early summer, the Mole and the Rat were just finishing breakfast when a heavy knock sounded at the door.

The Mole went to answer, and the Rat heard him utter a cry of surprise. The Mole exclaimed, "It's Mr. Badger!"

It was a surprising thing indeed that the Badger would visit anyone. The Badger strode heavily into the parlor. He looked at the two with utter seriousness.

"The hour has come!" he announced.

"What hour?" asked the Rat uneasily.

"Toad's hour!" replied the Badger. "I said I would take care of him as soon as the winter was over. You must accompany me to Toad Hall."

"Hooray!" cried the Mole. "*We'll* teach him to be a sensible Toad!"

When they reached the driveway of Toad Hall, they saw a large new car. As they neared the house, the front door flew open and out came Toad dressed in his new driving clothes.

"Hello! Come on!" he cried cheerfully. "You're just in time to come for a—er—for a . . . ." Toad stopped chattering when he saw the stern looks on the faces of his friends.

Badger strode up the steps. "Take him inside," he said to Rat and Mole. They grabbed Toad by the arms and hustled him through the door.

"You knew it would come to this sooner or later, Toad," the Badger explained severely. "You've ignored warnings from the police. You're wasting the money your father left you. All these wrecks you've had are dangerous, to yourself and to everyone else. We must talk."

Badger led Toad firmly into the library, and closed the door. Rat and Mole made themselves comfortable outside. Through the closed door they could hear the drone of Badger's voice. Later came the sound of Toad, sobbing.

Three-quarters of an hour later, the door opened. Badger reappeared, leading by the paw a very dejected Toad.

"Sit down there, Toad," said the Badger kindly. "Are you sorry for what you have done?"

There was a long, long pause. Toad looked all around, while the others waited in silence. At last, he spoke.

"No!" he said stoutly. "I'm *not* sorry. It was *fun!*"

The Badger fumed. "Very well, if you won't yield to reason, we'll have to try force. Toad, you've often asked us to stay in this handsome house of yours. Well, now we're going to. Take him upstairs, you two, and lock him in his bedroom."

"It's for your own good, Toady," said the Rat kindly, as he and the Mole hauled the Toad up the stairs. They thrust Toad into his room and locked the door.

"I've never seen Toad so determined," the Badger said. "He must never be left unguarded, not till this madness is over."

They agreed to take turns sleeping in Toad's room. At first Toad was very annoying. He would arrange the bedroom chairs in the shape of a motor car and crouch on them, pretending to drive. Then he would suddenly shout "Crash!", somersault, and lie on the floor amid the upturned chairs.

As time passed, these seizures became less and less violent. But Toad did not seem interested in anything else, and he became depressed and listless.

One fine morning the Rat went upstairs. "How are you today, Toady?" he asked as he approached Toad's bedside.

"O," moaned the Toad. "I've been such a bother. I mustn't ask you to do me a favor."

"I'd do anything for you, Toad, if only you'd be sensible."

"If I thought that, Ratty, I'd beg you to go to the village and get the doctor," whispered the Toad.

The Rat was alarmed. "Are you sick, Toady?" The Toad was very still, and moaned pitifully. "You *are* sick!"

The Rat patted the Toad's paw. "Don't you worry. I'll be back in a blink of an eye." He left Toad's bed, locked the bedroom door, and ran for the doctor's house.

As soon as he heard the key turn in the lock, Toad jumped lightly out of bed. He dressed in his best suit and took a bundle of cash from his bureau. Then he tied the bedsheets into a rope, knotted an end to the bed, and scrambled out the window.

Rat was gloomy when he had to admit to Badger and Mole that he had been fooled.

"But there's no sense in talking," said the Badger. "Toad's gotten away, who knows where. We'd better stay here. He may be back any time—on a stretcher, or between two policemen."

Meanwhile, Toad was feeling very proud of himself. Merry and irresponsible, he walked briskly along a road some miles from home.

Soon he reached an inn. He went inside and ordered the best luncheon available.

Halfway through his meal he heard a familiar sound. He trembled with joy. It was the sound of a motor car. He heard it stop. The inn's door opened, and the car's passengers entered, talkative and happy. Toad slipped out quietly.

"There can't be any harm," he said to himself, "in just *looking* at it!"

The car stood in the middle of the yard. Toad inspected it carefully. Then his eyes lit up. "I wonder," he whispered, "if this sort of car *starts* easily?"

Before he knew it, he was cranking the handle.

"*Poop-poop!*" went the car, and once again Toad was possessed. As if in a dream, he found himself in the driver's seat. He swung the car onto the road. Faster and faster it went. As the car devoured the highway, Toad felt large. Again he was Toad the Terror, the lord of the lone trail.

"Let me see," said the Judge, peering down from his bench. "How can we get the attention of this ruffian? First, he has been found guilty of stealing a valuable motor car. Second, he has been found to be a danger to the public. Third, he has been rude to the police.

"Prisoner, stand up!" commanded the Judge. "This time you are going to jail."

Policemen put chains on Toad's feet and dragged him away. Soon a rusty key creaked in a lock, and Toad found himself in the dungeon of the best-guarded prison in the land.

Toad's Adventures

When Toad found himself in the dank dungeon, he flung himself on the floor and cried.

"This is the end of Toad, the popular and handsome Toad, the rich and kind Toad! What a stupid animal I have been!" he wailed. Thus he passed his days and nights for several weeks.

Toad was often visited by the jailer's daughter, a pleasant girl who helped her father with light chores. Pitying poor Toad, she said to her father one day: "Father! The poor beast is so unhappy, and getting so thin. Please let me take care of him."

Her father replied that she could do what she liked. He was tired of Toad and his sulking. So that day she knocked at the door of Toad's cell.

"Now sit up, Toad," she coaxed, "and do try to eat something." The fragrance of tea and toast revived Toad. He ate a little, and soon felt much better.

He and the girl had many interesting talks together. The girl thought that it was a shame that Toad was locked up in prison, since he was not a bad sort of animal. One morning she came to Toad's cell, deep in thought.

"Toad," she said slowly, "I have an aunt who is a washerwoman. If you gave her some money, she might bring you a dress and bonnet. You could put them on, pretend you are her, and escape."

The next evening, the girl ushered her aunt into Toad's cell. In return for some gold coins, Toad received a cotton gown, an apron, a shawl, and a black bonnet.

Shaking with laughter, the girl and her aunt buttoned Toad into the dress, draped the shawl on his shoulders, and tied the bonnet under his chin.

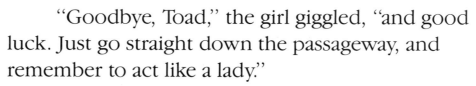

"Goodbye, Toad," the girl giggled, "and good luck. Just go straight down the passageway, and remember to act like a lady."

With a quaking heart, Toad pulled the bonnet low over his face and stepped down the corridor. At every gate, the guards recognized the washerwoman's familiar cotton dress and they paid little attention to Toad. Before he knew it Toad was outside the prison, feeling the fresh air. He was free!

In the distance, Toad could hear the puffing of a train. Making his way to the station, he discovered a train ready to leave in the direction of his home. But at the ticket window, he remembered to his horror that he had left his money in his cell.

Full of despair, Toad wandered down the platform. He knew his escape would soon be discovered.

Tears trickled down his nose. As he walked along, he found himself next to the engine, which was being oiled and wiped by its affectionate driver.

"Hullo, my dear lady!" said the engine-driver, when he saw the forlorn Toad. "What's the trouble?"

"O, sir!" cried Toad, "I am a poor washerwoman, and I've lost all my money. I *must* get home somehow!"

"That's bad," said the engine-driver. "Must get home to your children?"

"O yes," sobbed Toad, "And they'll be hungry, and playing with matches. O dear, O dear!"

The engine-driver smiled kindly. "Engine-driving is a dirty job. If you'll wash a few shirts for me, I'll give you a ride on my engine."

The Toad scrambled into the cab of the engine. "When I get

back to Toad Hall, I'll send the engine-driver enough money to pay for a whole pile of washing," he thought.

The whistle blew, and the train moved out of the station. As their speed increased, Toad could see fields, and trees, and cows, all flying past him. He was happy to think how every minute was bringing him closer to his home and his friends. He began to skip and sing. The engine-driver had met washerwomen before, but none like this.

They covered many miles, and the sun set and a brightly shining moon rose. Suddenly, cocking his ear, the driver leaned far out the window. He looked behind them. "Strange," he said. "There's another train behind us! And the engine is crowded with policemen, waving at us to stop!"

Terrified, Toad fell to his knees. "O save me, kind sir!" he begged. "I am not what I seem. I am a toad. If they capture me, they will put me in chains. I just wanted to borrow a car. I didn't mean to steal it, really."

The engine-driver looked very stern. He said, "You have been a very bad toad. But the sight of an animal in tears is too much. I will help you.

"Ahead is a long tunnel. We will speed through it, but the other train will slow down in the dark. When we are through the tunnel, I will put on the brakes as hard as I can. You must jump off and hide in the woods while they chase me!"

They piled coal into the engine, and the train roared into the tunnel. Then they were on the other side, in the fresh air and moonlight. The driver put on the brakes, and the train screeched to a crawl. Toad heard him call, "Now! Jump!"

Toad jumped, rolled down an embankment, and, unhurt, scrambled into the woods. The train picked up speed and was gone. Then out of the tunnel burst the other train, roaring and whistling, its crew waving their nightsticks. It flashed past Toad's hiding place and disappeared.

After he stopped laughing, Toad realized that it was cold and dark. He was far from home, with no money. He found a hollow tree, made a bed of dry leaves, curled up, and slept soundly till morning.

The Further Adventures of Toad

Toad woke up early. Sitting up, he rubbed his eyes first and his cold toes next. He wondered where he was. Then with a leap of his heart, he remembered everything—remembered his escape, remembered the train ride, remembered that he was free!

Free! The word and the thought alone were worth fifty blankets. Warm now, he shook himself, and marched forth into the sun, hungry but hopeful.

After some miles, Toad reached a main road. Far in the distance he saw a motor car approaching. Hoping for a ride, Toad stepped into the road. Suddenly, his knees turned to water and he collapsed. The car was the same one that he had stolen at the inn!

The motor car stopped next to him, and two gentlemen jumped out. One of them called to the two women in the car, "How sad! This poor woman has fainted! Let's take her into town; she must have friends there." The men tenderly lifted Toad into the back seat and proceeded on their way.

Toad drifted back to his senses, knowing that he had not been recognized. He cautiously opened one eye and then the other.

"Look!" said one of the men. "She is better already. How do you feel?"

"Thank you kindly, sir," said Toad in a feeble voice. "I'm feeling much better. If I could sit in front, next to the driver, with the air on my face, I would soon be all right."

They carefully helped Toad into the front seat. Toad tried to beat down the old urges that he was feeling.

"Please, sir," he said, "I've been watching you carefully. Can I drive? I'd like to be able to tell my friends that I drove a motor car!"

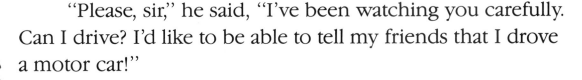

Before anyone knew it, Toad had taken the wheel. At first he drove slowly. "Be careful, washerwoman!" the others called out. This annoyed Toad.

"Washerwoman?" he cried, as the car leaped to full speed. "No! I am the Toad, the Toad who always escapes! Sit still, and you shall know what driving really is!"

With a cry of horror, the others all tried to take the wheel, but the Toad sent the car crashing through a hedge. One mighty bound, and the car splashed into a muddy pond. Toad flew through the air and landed on his back with a thump, in the soft, rich grass of a meadow. Sitting up, he saw the car in the pond, nearly submerged. Its four occupants were floundering angrily in the water.

Toad picked himself up and ran as hard as he could across the meadow. In the distance he could hear shouting and the wail of a police siren. Crashing through the brush, he suddenly realized that there was no earth beneath his feet. *Splash*! He had run straight into the River!

He rose to the surface, tossed this way and that by the current. Struggling, he saw he was being carried toward a dark hole in the bank. As the water swept him past, Toad reached out and grabbed the edge of the hole. With the last of his strength, he pulled himself out of the water.

As he rested, he saw some bright, small thing twinkling in the hole, moving towards him. A face gradually appeared around them—a small, brown face, with whiskers, neat little ears, and silky hair.

It was the Rat!

Away from Home

The Rat gripped Toad by the scruff of the neck, and hauled his waterlogged friend into the hallway. Toad was overjoyed to be in the house of a friend.

"O, Ratty!" he cried. "I've been through such sufferings since I saw you last! Been in prison—escaped, of course! O, I *am* a smart Toad!"

"Toad," said the Rat sternly, "you go take off that dress and clean up right now. I have never seen such a sorry sight. Stop bragging, and go!"

When Toad returned, the Rat spoke. "Don't you see what a fool you've been making of yourself? Was it fun being in prison? Do you think it would be fun to break your neck in an accident?"

"I'm going to change my ways," said Toad. "Now I'm going to be a good Toad. I have an idea. We'll stroll over to Toad Hall and—"

"Stroll over to Toad Hall!?" cried the Rat. "Haven't you heard?"

"Heard what?" said Toad, turning rather pale.

The Rat's voice was low. "When we heard you were in prison, Badger and Mole moved to Toad Hall to keep things in order. But the weasels and the ferrets from the Wild Wood heard, too. They came in the night, dozens of them. They beat Mole and

Badger and took over the house. The Wild Wooders have been there ever since, eating all the food, breaking everything, and making jokes about you."

Just then there was a knock, and in walked Badger and Mole. The Badger looked tired, and his feet were covered in mud. The Mole was tired too, and he slumped into a chair.

"What's it like out there?" asked the Rat.

"About as bad as can be," the Mole replied. "There are guards everywhere."

The Badger walked past them and stood before the fireplace, thinking deeply. The other three sat down and did not speak. Toad was on the sofa, with his legs up and his face buried in his knees. He was sobbing.

"Cheer up, Toady!" said the Badger. "We're not done yet. I'm going to tell you a secret."

Toad sat up slowly and dried his eyes. Secrets were a great attraction to him, because he could never keep one.

"*There is a secret underground passage!*" said the Badger impressively. "Your father told me about it many years ago, and asked me to keep it a secret until you had need of it. The secret tunnel leads from the river bank up into the pantry in the kitchen of Toad Hall."

Toad brightened. "But how can it help us?" he asked.

"I've found out today," continued the Badger, "that there's going to be a banquet at Toad Hall tomorrow night. It's the Chief Weasel's birthday. All the weasels will be in the banquet hall, eating and drinking and carrying on. They will suspect nothing."

"We shall jump out of the pantry—" cried the Mole.

"—with our pistols and our sticks—" cried the Rat.

"—and whack 'em and whack 'em and whack 'em!" shouted the Toad gleefully.

"Very well, then," said the Badger, "our plan is settled. It's getting very late, so let's go to bed at once. We'll be ready tomorrow."

The Return of the Heroes

The next evening, when it began to grow dark, the Rat summoned the other three into the parlor. He then dressed them for their adventure. First, there was a belt for each animal, and a sword to hang from it. Then everyone received a pistol, a policeman's billy club, several sets of handcuffs, and a lunchbox full of sandwiches.

When everyone was ready, the Badger said, "Now then, follow me! And Toady! Don't chatter, or we'll leave you behind!"

The Badger led them along the River for a little way. Then he suddenly swung himself into a hidden hole in the river bank, a little above the water. The others followed.

Inside the tunnel it was cold, and damp, and low, and narrow. Listening for any sound, they shuffled along, their paws on their pistols. The Badger led them for some time, and then stopped. "We should be under Toad Hall now," he whispered.

Above them, somewhere, there was a murmur of sound—a confused sound of shouting and cheering and stamping on the floor.

"What a time they are having!" said the Badger. "Come on!" They hurried along the tunnel until they found themselves standing under a trap door.

The weasels were making a tremendous racket. The four friends put their shoulders to the trap door and heaved it back. Hoisting each other up, they found themselves standing in the pantry. Only a door separated them from the banquet hall.

The noise was deafening. The weasels were cackling, and throwing dishes against the walls.

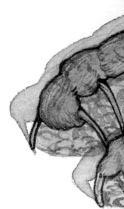

The Badger stood tall, and firmly gripped his stick with both paws. He glanced at his friends and cried—

"The hour has come! Follow me!" And he flung the door open wide.

My!

Squealing and squeaking filled the air! The terrified weasels dove this way and that. Ferrets rushed into the fireplace. Tables and chairs were knocked over, and dishes crashed to the floor.

The enemy was thrown into a panic when the four heroes rushed into the room! There was the mighty Badger, his whiskers bristling, swinging his club through the air. And the Mole, black and grim, waving his stick. And the Rat, desperate and determined, his belt bulging with every kind of weapon. And the Toad, puffed to twice his normal size, leaping into the air and whooping. There were only four of them, but to the panic-stricken weasels the room seemed full of attacking animals.

The weasels scrambled and tried to flee, through the windows, up the chimney, anywhere. In five minutes the room was cleared. On the floor lay a dozen of the enemy, whom the Rat was busy handcuffing. The Badger leaned on his stick and wiped his brow.

The Mole jumped out the window and chased after the last terrified weasels. Soon he returned. "It's all over," he reported. "They're all gone, and I've got their rifles."

"Excellent!" said the Badger. "Now, let's make these prisoners clean up the place."

Working double-time, the remaining weasels cleaned Toad Hall from top to bottom. They said they were very sorry for what they had done, and were grateful when the Mole gave them each a dinner roll and let them go.

That night the four friends slept between clean sheets, safe in Toad's ancient home, won back by their bravery.

The next night everyone from the River was invited to a banquet of celebration at Toad Hall.

All the animals cheered when Toad entered the hall. They gathered around to congratulate him and praise his cleverness and courage. But the Toad only smiled faintly and murmured, "Not at all! Badger was the mastermind, and Rat and Mole were far braver than I." No one had ever seen the Toad so modest. He was indeed a changed Toad!

After this adventure, the four animals continued to lead their lives in great joy and contentment. Toad sent a gold chain and locket to the jailer's daughter. He also thanked and rewarded the engine-driver, and repaid the owner of the car that he had driven into the pond.

Sometimes, during the long summer evenings, the four friends would stroll together in the Wild Wood. It was now tame as far as they were concerned. The mother weasels would bring their children to the mouths of their holes, and say, "Look! There goes the famous Mr. Mole! And the brave Water Rat, walking with him. And the great Mr. Toad!" And when the infants were bad, the mother weasels warned that if they were not good, the gray Badger would come and get them. This was an unfair thing to say. For although he shied away from social life, the Badger, you see, was rather fond of children.

THE END

Text © 1993 by Running Press
Illustrations © 2001, 1993 by Don Daily

9 8 7 6 5 4 3 2 1
Digit on the right indicates the number of this printing

Library of Congress Cataloging-in-Publication Number 93-070550
ISBN 0-7624-0999-1

Cover and interior design by Nancy Loggins Gonzalez
Typography: ITC Garamond by Richard Conklin

This book may be ordered by mail from the publisher.
Please include $2.50 for postage and handling.
But try your bookstore first!

Published by Courage Books, an imprint of
Running Press Book Publishers
125 South Twenty-second Street
Philadelphia, Pennsylvania 19103-4399

Visit us on the web!
www.runningpress.com